Tales from Brierybank

Rocking Chair Stories

Easy to Read
Selected by Meg Daniels

GEDDES & GROSSET

Published by Geddes & Grosset, an imprint of
Children's Leisure Products Limited

© 1997 Children's Leisure Products Limited,
David Dale House, New Lanark ML11 9DJ, Scotland

First published 1997
Reprinted 1999

ISBN 1 85534 186 7

Printed and bound in India

Contents

Long Live Their Majesties

Their Majesties Wash Up

The King of Pennidip came cheerfully down to breakfast, kissed the Queen good morning and turned the radio on.

"Sque-e-e-e, pip-pop, gurgle," said the radio for it was quite an old radio.

The King twiddled the knobs.

"Tum-te-tiddley-um-te-tum," said the radio, beginning to play the "Teddy Bears' Picnic".

"Oh, that reminds me," said the King; "talking of

picnics, I've just told the servants they can have the day off. They wanted to go for a picnic in the woods so I said it would be all right."

"Oh, did you?" said the Queen, pouring him out his tea with not nearly enough sugar in it. "Well, I hope you like washing up, that's all."

"Why, what do you mean?" asked the King, stirring his tea with so much clanking and rattling of the spoon that the Queen took it away from him.

"There was a large and elaborate banquet last night," said the Queen.

"I know," said the King, who had eaten too much.

"The kitchen is full of dishes and things waiting to be washed up," went on the Queen. "And now you've gone and let all the servants go to a picnic, we shall have to do it ourselves."

"But I've got to do simply lots of ruling this morning," said the King.

"You've got to do simply lots of washing up this morning," said the Queen, spreading the marmalade twice as thick as was necessary. "The ruling can wait, the washing up cannot. We can very well do without any new laws for a bit, but we can't do without any clean plates and cups."

Her Majesty put on a little apron with pink daisies embroidered on it, tied the King up in a heavy overall and carted him out to the kitchen.

"Wow!" exclaimed His Majesty when he saw the dirty dishes. There were simply towers of them. Cartloads of cups and piles of plates. Showers of saucers, stacks of spoons and a great many glasses.

The Queen turned on the hot tap and everywhere was immediately full of steam.

"Come on, Kingy!" she cried, splashing away in the washing-up bowl.

"Oh, bother!" said the King, getting down the drying-up cloth.

Then there was silence for some time except for a slight crash when the King dropped a plate.

"Here," said the King after they had been washing up and drying up for simply ages. "How many more things are there?"

"Not many, nearly finished now," said the Queen, floating a little basin on the washing-up water.

"Well, I didn't know we had as many as a hundred and fifty teacups with pink roses on them," said the King.

"Neither we have," said the Queen, sinking the little basin with a dab of the washing-up mop and beginning to fish up spoons by the handful. "We had twenty-four but one of the maids broke two and one is on the dresser with ten-penny pieces in it for the baker. You borrowed one to mix gold paint in, to paint that cardboard crown that you wear indoors to save your proper one. That makes twenty left."

"Well," said the King, scratching his head and forgetting he had a bunch of forks in his hand, which scratched it harder than he meant, "I've been counting them and I've dried up a hundred and fifty already and there are still plenty more to do. Why, ow, oo-er, good gracious, magic, impossible!" he exclaimed, going all of a dither.

"What's the matter?" asked the Queen, clapping down five fine fish forks and a handful of soapsuds.

"Look!" cried the King, pointing to the table where he'd been putting the dried-up things. "I've dried up a hundred and fifty teacups and there are only six there. Where are the others? Vanished! Disappeared! The Palace must be haunted. Oh-oh, help, I'm scared!"

"Fiddlesticks!" snapped the Queen. She looked round. Then she too gave a gasp and came over all frightened.

"Why, wherever can they be?" she cried, "and how did you dry up a hundred and fifty cups when we haven't got anything like so many?"

"There you are," said the King, "I told you the Palace was haunted. Cups wouldn't disappear by themselves if it weren't."

He put down a cup he had just dried and they both stared hard at it.

"Go on, disappear," said the King.

But the cup just stayed visible. Nothing happened at all.

"Let's look away for a moment and perhaps it will vanish," said the Queen. "They say a watched pot never boils, so perhaps a watched cup never disappears."

They looked away, counted ten and looked back. The cup was still there.

Just then in came the Lord Chamberlain.

"The Palace is haunted," said the King. "Things disappear." They told him about the mysterious business of the cups.

"I know," said the Lord Chamberlain, "I'll hide in a cupboard while you go on with the washing up, then perhaps I shall see where the things disappear to."

"Good idea," said the King. So the Lord Chamberlain squeezed himself into a cupboard which took some doing as the cupboard was a skinny one and rather full of shelves, while the Lord Chamberlain was rather fat and very full of breakfast. But at last he got himself packed in and watched through the keyhole while the royal washing-up began again.

The King dried up five more cups and three plates.

Suddenly the Lord Chamberlain gave a shout and burst out of the cupboard with a loud pop, like a cork out of a bottle.

"I see it!" he cried, "I see it. Oh, ha, ha, ha, he, he, he, it's ever so funny."

"Is it?" said the Queen, not thinking it was.

"Oh yes, ha, ha, ha, I understand it all now," roared the Lord Chamberlain.

"Well, tell us then!" cried the King, stamping his foot so firmly that two large dishes came apart in the Queen's hands.

"Well—er, there isn't any magic about it," said the Lord Chamberlain, calming down. "You kept washing up the same things over and over again."

"What do you say?" gasped the King.

"Yes, I'll explain," said the Lord Chamberlain. "You see, when your Majesty dried a cup you put it on this table. Then when the Queen had washed up a few things and went to take more, she started taking the ones you had already dried up, but didn't notice that was what she was doing."

"And so we kept on washing and drying the same things over and over again," said the Queen.

"No wonder there seemed to be an awful lot," said the King.

"Ha, ha, very funny," said the Queen. Then she turned to the Lord Chamberlain. "You are very

clever to find it out," she said. "Now you can be still more clever and help us to finish the rest of the washing up."

But the Lord Chamberlain was cleverer than that and he managed to persuade the Queen to leave the rest of the washing up until the servants came back from their picnic.

"Next time you give everyone the day off to go to a picnic," said the Queen to the King, "you can do the washing up by yourself."

"No fear," said the King. "I shall go to the picnic with them."

The Truthful Parrot

Once upon a time there was a poor farmer who owned a very beautiful parrot. Its feathers were green with tufts of blue, yellow and red. It had learned to talk very well, but it had a habit of always speaking the truth.

Now the farmer's wife was not a bad woman, but she sometimes did things she did not want anyone to know about, but the parrot was always watching and quite able to tell what it had seen!

Though he worked hard, the farmer never earned much money and his wife got rather tired of always eating rice and vegetables. So they were both quite excited one evening when the husband brought home a small chicken which had been given to him.

"Cook it tomorrow," he said, "and eat half of it yourself. I will have the rest for my supper."

The chicken was a great treat. The woman

thoroughly enjoyed her portion, but it was such a little bit! So she took a little more, and a little more, till she had finished it all.

When her husband came home at night, she said, "Oh, such a disaster! A stray cat came in while I was out and ate up your piece of chicken."

"You ate it yourself! You know you did!" cried the parrot, fluttering its wings excitedly.

Of course the woman was very angry and called the parrot a liar. Then she said to her husband, "I won't stand it any longer. Either you get rid of that wicked bird or part with me."

"Oh, please don't kill me!" sobbed the parrot. "Suppose you put me in a cage covered with a coloured cloth and take me to the market. You might sell me for quite a lot of money. Only promise to let me fix my own price."

The farmer agreed and took the bird to the market the very next day. He spent hours walking about, shouting, "Who'll buy? Who'll buy?" But those who would buy offered too low a price to please the parrot.

"Carry me to the Palace gardens," it said, "we may have better luck there."

And so it turned out, for someone saw them from a window and asked them in, and they were admitted at once to see the King.

When the parrot saw where it was, it made a very low bow, and cried "Greetings!"

The King was delighted.

"What is the price of this bird?" he asked.

"Ten thousand silver coins," replied the parrot promptly.

"That's a lot of money," said the King, but he ordered it to be paid and the farmer went home, feeling very rich.

The parrot lived in fine style. It had a silver cage, a silver drinking cup and was fed on fruits and sweetmeats. Everyone in the Palace petted it, and the King himself often sent for it to chat with him. However, the parrot's dearest friend was little Joya, the slave girl, whose duty it was to give it fresh seed and water every day.

One day the Court ladies amused themselves by asking the parrot's opinion of their looks. The parrot replied, telling one she was charming, another beautiful, a third that she had nice eyes, and so on. Then came the King's aunt who was very fat.

"What do you think of me?" she asked.

"Oh, you are not at all pretty," replied the parrot, "you look just like a pig."

The Court ladies sniggered, but the King's aunt waddled away looking very angry.

Last of all came little Joya and whispered, "Am I pretty too?"

"You would be," the parrot replied, "if you were to wash your face and to wear a pearl necklace."

The King's aunt was so angry to hear that even a slave girl with a dirty face was pretty, that she demanded that the parrot's neck should be wrung at once.

Now, the King was very fond of the parrot, and besides, he had paid a high price for it. So he begged for a week's delay, before the execution should take place.

Soon everyone in the palace knew that the parrot was under sentence of death, but no one was more upset than poor Joya. When she had said a tearful "Goodnight" to the bird, she added very softly, "Remember, I have forgotten to fasten your cage door, and the window is open too."

The parrot took the hint, and when the Palace was quiet for the night, it hopped out of its cage and flew away. In spite of its wings being stiff through lack of use, it reached the outskirts of the city and settled down for the night in an old garden. With the first streak of dawn, it flew towards the seashore.

Soon, to its great delight, it came upon a large flock of parrots that appeared to be flying out to sea.

"Oh! do wait for me, and tell me where you are going," the parrot cried.

The parrots replied that they were going to a magic island they often visited, where the trees were not only laden with ripe fruit all the year round, but some bore sweetmeats as well.

"The shores are covered with pearls as big as eggs," added one parrot, "and no one lives there but a lovely, kind Princess who was kidnapped by a magician."

The parrot found the island even more beautiful, and the Princess even lovelier and kinder than it had expected. When the other parrots flew away, it asked if it could stay behind with the Princess. A long time passed, and the Princess and the parrot became very friendly. Still, the bird always remembered the Palace, and its little friend Joya, and sometimes it felt very sad.

One morning, seeing the parrot so low-spirited, the Princess asked what was the matter.

"I am thinking of Joya," replied the parrot.

"I am afraid you love her more than me," said the Princess, a trifle hurt.

The Parrot hung its head. "Yes, I do," it said. "I love her better than anyone else in the world, and I really feel that I must go and see her. But I promise faithfully I will come back if you will let me go, for I do love you too, Princess."

The Princess, seeing that the parrot yearned to go, agreed to the plan, and even strung a necklace of pearls for it to take as a present to the little slave girl.

Early the next morning the parrot set out, carrying the necklace in its beak. After having flown some distance and feeling rather tired of carrying the pearls, it thought it would lay them for a minute on a small black rock which stuck out of the water. But alas! it was not a rock at all but a big fish which opened its mouth and swallowed the necklace.

The parrot wanted to cry, but plucking up courage, it flew back to the island and told the Princess of its bad luck. The good-natured Princess soon strung some more pearls and the parrot set out once more.

This time it reached the shore safely, and was just thinking how well everything was going when a wolf jumped out of a bush and called out "Stop thief! Stop thief!"

"I'm *not* a thief!" the parrot cried indignantly. Of course, when it opened its beak to speak, it dropped the pearls, and the wolf snapped them up and ran off. The poor parrot was so upset that this time it did cry. However, it was so anxious to give Joya a necklace that again it flew back to the island, and again the kind Princess made another necklace. This time, she twisted it round and round the parrot's neck, and both of them wondered why they had not thought of this plan before. The parrot arrived at the Palace safely, but took care not to approach it until it was dark. But Joya welcomed the parrot quite openly and soon explained that the King's aunt had gone a long, long way off, to live in a far distant country. Now there was no need for the parrot to fear having its neck wrung.

The King was delighted to welcome back his lost pet, and ordered the daintiest refreshments—oranges, melons and delicious iced sherbet to be served to it. Also Joya prepared a bath of scented water in a silver bowl. After the parrot had feasted and bathed, the King sent for it, and sat up till dawn, listening to its adventures and its description of the magic island and the lovely Princess. Before morning, the King had quite made up his mind to sail to the island, rescue the Princess, and beg her to marry him. A fine ship was prepared, built of oak and ivory and with sails of sea-green silk.

The King and the Princess fell in love with each other at first sight, for she was even more beautiful than the parrot had described her.

She told him of the cruel magician who had carried her off and threatened to keep her on the island until someone offered to marry her. As no one but parrots ever came there, the poor Princess said she had given up hope of being rescued until she caught sight of the royal ship's sea-green sails.

The homeward journey was quickly made, and the wedding of the King and the Princess soon took place with great splendour.

There were crowds of guests, all in the most gorgeous clothes. Even Joya kept looking at herself in all the mirrors, because she had a new scarlet robe and the parrot's pearls round her brown neck.

But the King in cloth of gold and the Princess in silver silk outshone them all. The parrot sat on a silver perch at the King's right hand.

"Our Queen is the dearest creature in the world, isn't she?" whispered the happy King to the parrot.

"I'm glad you think so, sir," replied the truthful parrot, "but I still like Joya best of all."

Pinocchio

How Pinocchio was Made

Once upon a time a man found a piece of wood lying in the forest and took it home.

"What a fine piece of wood!" he said. "I will make it into a table leg."

So he took his axe and had just begun to cut it when a voice said:

"Do not hit me so hard!"

The man did not know who had spoken. He looked round the room but could not see anyone. So he

took his axe and began again. But each time he tried to cut the wood it spoke to him. At last he was very glad to give it to a little old man who lived near. The name of the little man was Geppetto and he was very poor.

"I will make a puppet from this wood," he said to himself. "Then I will take it round the countryside and people will come and see it."

A puppet is a wooden doll that can be made to dance and do tricks.

So Geppetto took his tools and began to carve the log of wood. At last it was done, and was shaped just like a boy.

"I will call this little puppet Pinocchio!" said Geppetto. "That will be a good name for him."

As soon as the puppet was finished, he began to move his hands just like a real boy. Then Geppetto took Pinocchio and began to teach him to walk and then to walk and run, just like a real boy.

Round and round the room he went, then away he ran out of the door.

Geppetto ran after him but could not catch him. Everyone stared at the little wooden puppet running away down the street, chased by a little old man.

Just then some people who knew Geppetto came by.

"Poor little puppet!" they said to each other. "Geppetto is not kind to him and he's running away. We will put that bad Geppetto in prison for the night."

So they took the poor little man away to prison and the puppet ran home.

When Pinocchio got indoors he was very tired and soon fell asleep by the fire. While he was sleeping, he did not know that his feet were too close to the fire. After a while they began to burn because they were made of wood, and soon he had no feet left.

Next morning Geppetto came home. He was very upset to see his poor puppet with no feet and set to work to make him two lovely new feet. Pinocchio felt much better then and said:

"I am so sorry I was a bad boy. I will be good now and will do just what you tell me. I will even go to school and learn all my lessons if you want me to."

How Pinocchio Went to School

Next day as he ran along the road to school, Pinocchio heard a band playing in the distance, and stopped to listen. "I will go and hear the band play today," he decided, "and tomorrow I will go to school."

So away he ran until he came to a fairground. In a big tent there was a puppet show, and in went Pinocchio.

One of the puppets on the stage saw Pinocchio and called out:

"There is our brother Pinocchio. Come up here, dear brother."

The little puppet felt very proud and ran quickly on to the stage.

They were so glad to see Pinocchio, they came closer and hugged and kissed him, and soon the showman had him dancing with the rest.

When the show was over Pinocchio was given five golden pieces of money to take home to his father.

Pinocchio was delighted. He put the money in his pocket and set off for home as fast as he could go.

But he had not gone very far when he met a fox and a cat. The fox was lame and the cat was blind, so they were helping each other along.

The fox spoke to the little puppet, and when Pinocchio jingled the coins in his pocket, he made

up his mind to have them. He told Pinocchio that he knew of a wonderful field in the Land of the Owls.

"If you plant your money in this field in the middle of the night," he said, "it will grow into a tree covered in money."

When foolish little Pinocchio agreed to do this, the fox and the cat left him. Then, in the middle of the night, Pinocchio set off alone for the magic field.

It was very dark and on the way he was chased by two robbers who asked him for his money. They were the fox and the cat dressed up in black sacks, so Pinocchio did not recognize them.

But he had hidden the money in his mouth and the robbers could not find it. So they hung him up on a tree and ran away.

Happily a kind fairy had pity on the little puppet and took him home with her.

Pinocchio was sorry he had been so foolish, but he still did silly things and naughty things too. Worst of all, he did not tell the truth.

To punish him the fairy made his nose grow longer each time he told a lie. It grew so long that at last he could not get out of the door.

Poor Pinocchio was very upset and cried for a long

time and promised from then on he would tell the truth always. So the little fairy called up a thousand woodpeckers and they pecked his nose until it was the right size again.

The happy puppet then set off to find his father. He had not gone very far, however, when he met the fox and the cat again. They still wanted to get his money and asked him once more to come to the magic field in the Land of the Owls.

At first Pinocchio would not listen, but at last he agreed to go with them, and forgot all about his father.

When they reached the field, Pinocchio planted his money just as they told him. Then he went away to wait for the tree to grow. By the time he came back the bad fox and the cat had stolen all his money.

Now that he was poor and hungry, Pinocchio wandered from place to place until one day he met a little old woman. She asked him to help carry her load of firewood and promised him something nice to eat in return.

Pinocchio agreed and when they got to her home, he was given a fine meal which he ate hungrily. When Pinocchio looked up to thank the old woman

he found to his amazement that she had turned into his friend the fairy.

Pinocchio was so happy, especially when the fairy told him that if he was good, he would turn into a real boy one day.

So the next day Pinocchio went to school. He worked so hard, he began to be quite a clever puppet.

How Pinocchio Found Geppetto

In the school there were one or two boys who were very lazy, and Pinocchio often played with them.

One day one of these lazy boys, who was called Candlewick, told Pinocchio he was going to a place called the Land of Boobies. He said there were no schools in that land and boys could play all day.

So the silly puppet listened to him, and off they

went to the Land of Boobies. There they found many other boys who played all day long and did no lessons.

Pinocchio soon forgot all about his father and the little fairy. He forgot all his lessons too. Then one day he woke up to find he had grown a donkey's ears. Candlewick had donkey's ears too. Worse still, by and by they both turned into real donkeys.

One day a man came along and said to them:

"All boys who will not do lessons grow into donkeys and so they must work like donkeys."

So the foolish Pinocchio had to work all day just like a donkey, and sometimes was treated harshly by his cruel owner.

He next had to learn to do tricks for a grand show and one day, when he had to jump through a hoop, he was so tired, he fell and hurt his leg so badly that the vet said he would always be lame. So Pinocchio was sold to another owner.

This man did not want Pinocchio to work for him. He just wanted a donkey's skin to make a drum. Luckily Pinocchio escaped and swam far out to sea and turned into a puppet once more.

But in that part of the sea there was a very, very big

fish called a dogfish. He was so big he could even swallow people and ships.

So one minute Pinocchio was swimming along nicely, the next he found himself inside the dogfish!

At first he was afraid, and screamed. Then he looked round and saw a man sitting at a table. To his astonishment and delight he saw it was his father, Geppetto. The big fish had swallowed him too and he had been there so long he had made himself a table, a chair and other useful things from floating wreckage swallowed by the dogfish. He had also made friends with a tunny fish.

"We must get out of here," said Pinocchio to Geppetto and the tunny fish. "We must swim away this very night."

They waited until the dogfish was asleep, his mouth open so wide they could see the sky and the moon. Very quietly Pinocchio and Geppetto crept out of the dogfish and the tunny fish swam with them.

At first Pinocchio swam with Geppetto on his back. Then, when he got too tired, he climbed on the back of the tunny fish and helped his father up too. Then away swam the tunny towards the shore.

Safely ashore Pinocchio thanked the tunny fish and said goodbye to him. Then he and his father walked till at last they came upon a deserted hut where they settled in straight away.

How Pinocchio Became a Boy

The next morning, Pinocchio went to a farm to fetch some milk. As Pinocchio had no money, the farmer said to him:

"If you will pump me a hundred buckets of water I will give you a glass of milk."

Pinocchio was glad to do something to earn the milk, so every day he went to pump the water. It was very hard work, but he did not mind. He was growing into a very good and kind puppet. He also learnt to make baskets with grass and rushes, which he sold, and with the money he bought food for Geppetto and himself.

Pinocchio worked so hard that at last he was able to save enough money to buy himself a new coat, a new hat and new shoes.

On the way to buy them, however, he met a snail who told him that the good fairy was very ill and had nothing to eat.

"Take this money," said Pinocchio to the snail, "and give it to the fairy. I do not want new clothes now. I want the kind fairy to have the money."

That night Pinocchio sat up making baskets out of rushes until midnight.

"I am strong and I will work hard every day," he said to himself. "Then I can earn enough money for my dear father and for the fairy too."

When at last he did go to bed, he dreamt that the fairy came and kissed him.

When he awoke he had such a surprise. He was a

puppet no longer. He was a real, live boy with blue eyes and brown hair. And on his bed was a brand new suit of clothes.

Pinocchio had never been so happy in all his life. He dressed himself in his new clothes and ran into the next room to show himself to his father.

"Who has done all this?" asked Pinocchio.

"*You* have done it," said Geppetto. "When you were a puppet, you were often very bad. But now that you are trying to be good, you are a happy little boy, and I am happy too."

"How glad I am that I am not a puppet any more!" said Pinocchio. "It is much better to be a good little boy, than a bad little puppet."

King Benedict

Long, long ago, there was a king called King Benedict. He was young and handsome, and he was the best King that ever lived. All his people loved him and were very happy.

One day, the King was sitting on his Golden Throne, wondering what he could do to make all his people even happier, when suddenly he had an idea!

"It would be nice," he thought, "if I were to be married and have a wife; then she would be my Queen, and we could have lots of little boys and girls to be Princes and Princesses and all my people would then be even happier still."

He thought it was a very good idea, so he clapped his hands once, and in came the Royal Scribe carrying his Golden Pen. He bowed very low.

"Oh, King!" said the Royal Scribe, "is there something you wish to tell me?"

"Yes there is." said the King, "I've been wondering what I could do to make all my people even happier, and I've had an idea. Wouldn't it be nice if I were to be married and have a wife? Then she would be my Queen and we could have lots of little boys and girls to be Princes and Princesses and all my people would be even happier still.

"Oh, King!" said the Royal Scribe, "I think that's a very good idea. Shall we call in your two Royal Treasure Keepers, and see what *they* think?"

The King agreed, so he clapped his hands twice, and in came his two Royal Treasure Keepers, one behind the other, carrying their Golden Coins. They both bowed very low.

"Oh, King!" said the elder of the two Royal Treasure Keepers, "is there something you wish to tell us?"

"Yes," said the King, "there is," and he told them all about his idea.

"Oh, King!" said the elder of the two Royal Treasure Keepers, "we think that's a very good idea. Shall we call in your three Wise Old Men and see what *they* think?"

The King agreed, so he clapped his hands three times, and in came his three Wise Old Men, one behind the other, carrying their Golden Books. They all bowed very low.

"Oh, King!" said the oldest of the three Wise Old Men, "is there something you wish to tell us?"

"Yes," said the King, "there is," and he told them all about his idea.

"Oh, King!" said the oldest of the three Wise Old Men, "we think that's a very good idea. Shall we call in your four Gallant Generals and see what *they* think?"

The King agreed, so he clapped his hands four times, and in came his four Gallant Generals, one behind the other, carrying their Golden Swords. They all bowed very low.

"Oh, King!" said the oldest of the four Gallant Generals, "is there something you wish to tell us?"

"Yes," said the King, "there is," and he told them all about his idea.

"Oh, King!" said the oldest of the four Gallant Generals, "we think that's a very good idea, and it would indeed make all your people even happier."

The King was pleased, so they all bowed very low, and went out again.

First went the Four Gallant Generals, one behind the other, carrying their Golden Swords; then the three Wise Old Men, one behind the other, carrying their Golden Books; then the two Royal Treasure Keepers, one behind the other, carrying their Golden Coins, and last of all, the Royal Scribe, carrying his Golden Pen.

When they had all gone, the King decided to go hunting in the forest, so he rode out through the gates of the Palace on his beautiful white horse.

Outside the gates there was a young maiden selling flowers to all the people who had come to the city to see the King and the Royal Palace.

She was dressed all in rags, but she was very beautiful and was secretly in love with the King.

The following day, the King issued a Proclamation to every part of the Kingdom—the North, the South, the East and the West.

On Midsummer's Day, said the King's Proclamation, all the rich noblemen in every part of the Kingdom—the North, the South, the East and the West—were to bring their most beautiful daughter to the Royal Palace so that the King could choose one of them to be his Queen.

When that day came, and it was a beautiful day, all the rich noblemen from every part of the Kingdom—the North, the South, the East and the West—brought their most beautiful daughters to the city, and the King, dressed in his Royal robes, gave a magnificent party in the gardens of the Royal Palace. There were beautiful maidens from the North dressed in costly furs. There were beautiful maidens from the South dressed in precious silks. There were beautiful maidens from the East in dresses of shimmering satin, and there were beautiful maidens from the West wearing gowns of rich brocade. And all the beautiful maidens—from

the North, the South, the East and the West—fell deeply in love with the King.

There was one especially beautiful maiden from the North dressed in costly furs, and the King nearly fell in love with her, but alas! she had dark eyes, and the King didn't like dark eyes.

There was one especially beautiful maiden from the South dressed in precious silks, and the King nearly fell in love with her, but alas! she had black hair, and the King didn't like black hair.

There was one especially beautiful maiden from the East in a dress of shimmering satin, and the King nearly fell in love with her, but alas! she had pale cheeks, and the King didn't like pale cheeks.

Last of all, there was an especially beautiful maiden from the West wearing a gown of rich brocade, and the King nearly fell in love with her, but alas! she had a deep voice, and the King didn't like a deep voice.

The King was very sad, because there were so many beautiful maidens and yet he had not fallen in love with any of them.

Then, suddenly, he saw standing near the gates of the Royal Palace, the young maiden selling flowers.

She had beautiful blue eyes and soft golden hair. Her cheeks were like fresh roses, and her voice was like sweet music.

She was dressed all in rags, but she was the most beautiful maiden in the whole Kingdom, and the King fell instantly in love with her.

"I will ask this beautiful maiden to be my Queen," said the King.

The King, dressed in his finest robes, went down on one knee before her and asked her to be his Queen. She smiled sweetly and placed her hand in his, and the King rose, took her in his arms and kissed her, and promised to be kind and gentle to her as long as he lived.

The following day, the King sent his Golden Coach to bring her to the Palace and the Royal Seamstresses, with their Golden Needles, made her

beautiful dresses of costly furs, precious silks, shimmering satins and rich brocades.

Very soon the King and the beautiful maiden were married amid great rejoicing, and she became his Queen. They had lots of little boys and girls to be Princes and Princesses and they all lived happily ever after.

The Golden Mill

The Miller and his Wife

At an old water mill, that stood on the bank of a pretty river in the north country, there once lived a good miller named John. Besides the mill, he owned a cow, a horse and two or three fields by the waterside.

The cow gave him enough milk for himself and his wife, the horse drew his plough, and in his fields he planted corn, wheat and oats. This grain he ground into flour and meal, which lasted him all the year round.

"What more do I want?" he used to say. "Here I am, with enough to eat and drink as long as I live and a snug place to live in, even if it is only an old mill. It is my home and I would rather have it than the most splendid house in the world! I am not rich, but I would not change places with a king, no, not for sacks and sacks of gold!"

This good miller, even if he was not very well off, was very happy and content. He had a kind heart too and liked to see other people happy, as well as himself.

It always made him sad to hear of people who were sick or hungry or in trouble. He would often give some of his cow's rich, sweet milk went to sick children or old folks in the village near by. And many a poor man got his little store of corn or wheat ground into flour by the kindly miller, without having to pay a single penny.

"You will never be well off," Jean, his wife, used to say to him in a grumbling tone, "for you would give everything away if you got the chance. Now, I am not like you. I am not so foolish, I hope!"

Jean was not a bit like her husband. She would never have given anything to those who were worse off than she was.

Poor or needy folk never came to the mill when John was away from home. "It is no use," they would say; "we shall not get a drop or a crumb from the miller's wife. She is as mean as mean can be."

Jean kept a sharp eye on all her husband's corn and meal. And if she found that he had given any away, she would scold him sharply even when there was plenty to spare.

In twenty years or so, she had managed to save up a few gold crowns, which she kept in an old teapot on a high shelf. She never thought of spending any of the crowns or of giving them to some poor person. Each night when her work was done, she would take down the teapot and count the crowns over and over again. She liked doing this better than anything else.

"You say you would not change places with a king for sacks of gold," she said to John. "Well, I only wish I had some, that's all!"

The Wonderful Bowl

One night, just as John and his wife were about to go to bed, they heard a knock on the kitchen door.

Jean went to open it, and there stood a poor-looking woman in a green checked shawl. Her head and feet were bare, and in her hand she carried a small wooden bowl.

When she saw the miller's wife, she held out the bowl and said in a sweet voice:

"Would you be so kind, ma'am, as to fill this little bowl of mine with oatmeal?"

Jean looked her up and down. "How much will you pay me for it if I do?" she said.

"I have no money to pay you," said the woman. "But tomorrow you shall be paid back with another bowlful of meal."

"Oh, that's a fine tale!" said Jean. "I don't believe a word of it. You are a beggar, neither more nor less, and I will have no beggars here! Be off with you at once!"

She had almost shut the door in the woman's face when John came up behind her. "What is the matter?" he asked.

"Why," said Jean in an angry tone, "here's a strange beggar woman who wants her bowl filled with oatmeal. Does she think we have nothing else to do at the mill but to grind grain into meal for beggar folk? I should like to know how much meal we should have to make bread and porridge for ourselves, if we gave it away to every beggar who asked for it?"

"For shame, wife!" said the good miller. "As if we could not spare enough meal to fill a little bowl like that! Open the meal chest and fill the poor woman's bowl at once! I am the master of this mill. I grind the grain and I shall say what is to be done with it. Fill the bowl at once, I tell you!"

When the miller spoke in that way, his wife knew that it was no use to say anything more. But how she wished he had not been at home. Still, she took the wooden bowl, though with a very cross look, and carried it to the big meal chest in the corner of the kitchen.

Now the meal chest was nearly half full and Jean thought that a little meal would be enough to fill the bowl. But she soon found, to her great suprise, that it was the strangest bowl she had ever touched.

For try as she would, she could not fill it up with meal. She put in more and more, yet the bowl was not even half full. What could be the matter with it? She looked to see whether there was a hole in it, but no, the bowl had no holes or cracks in it. What a strange thing it was!

Another Strange Thing

Still Jean went on trying to fill the bowl and still it was not full, though the meal in the meal chest kept getting less and less. Eventually there was only a little meal in one corner. And yet the strange bowl was not nearly full.

At last, when there was not a bit of meal left in the chest, Jean went to the door and held out the bowl to the woman.

"Here," she said, "that's all I can give you."

"But," said the miller, who was looking on, "you have not filled the bowl. I told you to do so, Jean."

"Filled or not," said Jean, "I have emptied the meal chest into it, and you know yourself that the chest was half full. I have never seen such an odd bowl before! I believe that beggar is trying to play a trick on us. Send her off at once!"

"No," said the miller in a firm tone, "not until the bowl is full of meal. I said it should be filled for her and filled it shall be, even if every meal sack in the mill has to be emptied!"

As he spoke, John went into the mill to fetch one of his sacks of meal. He brought it back and set it down before his wife.

"Now," he said, "open that, and fill the poor woman's bowl."

So, with a very sulky face, Jean had to do as she was told. "There will not be a scrap of meal left for us if we go on at this rate," she grumbled, as she undid the string of the sack.

But lo and behold! She had no sooner taken out the first handful of oatmeal and put it into the little wooden bowl than it was filled to the very brim!

Jean stood and stared, but she was too full of wonder to speak a word. Instead, she just gave the bowl to the woman who took it and said:

"Thank you very much, good folk. You shall be paid back tomorrow with a bowl of meal, as I promised."

Then she went quietly away. Both John and Jean ran outside to see which way she went, for they both felt there was something very strange about their visitor. They looked all around them, this way and that, but the woman in the green checked shawl was nowhere to be seen.

The Boy in Green

For some time, Jean did nothing but grumble at the loss of her good oatmeal.

"I don't like such strange goings on," she said. "And I am sure that woman will never pay us back."

"Well, well, wife," said the miller, "if she does not, it will not matter at all. A mill can always spare a little meal now and again, and never miss it. And one should always do one's best for poor folk, you know."

Next day John rose early and went off to market, to a town some miles away. He would not be home until the next morning.

Jean was alone all day. She kept the doors locked, because she did not want any strange folk or beggars about the place.

"I know how to take care of what we have better than John does," she muttered to herself.

In the evening when her work was done, she reached down her old teapot from its high shelf. Then, sitting down by the fire, she began to count her gold crowns as she had done many a time before.

It had now grown dark, but Jean did not light any candles—she thought candles were a waste, when one could see just as well by firelight.

She got up to poke the fire into a blaze and nearly dropped her poker in surprise! For there, right in front of her on the hearthstone, stood a tiny boy!

How had he got there? The windows were shut tight and so was the door; and the miller's wife had not heard a sound. Had he slipped down the chimney or crept through a mousehole? Jean stared at him without a word.

He was no taller than her little three-legged stool and he was dressed from head to foot in green. It was just the same shade of green as the checked shawl of the woman who had been to the mill the night before. He had black hair, sparkling black eyes and two rows of shining teeth. In his hand he held a bowl filled to the brim with oatmeal. This he gave to Jean, saying in a very shrill, high voice:

"My mistress has sent you this meal, ma'am, to pay you back for what was given to her. You will find it very good."

"Who is your mistress?" asked Jean, staring more than ever as she took the bowl.

"The Queen of the Fairy Folk," said the little boy in green.

Just as he spoke, the logs on the hearthstone fell with a crash. There was a blaze of light and a shower of sparks. And when Jean looked again, the boy had gone.

Fairy Meal

Full of wonder, the miller's wife gazed round the kitchen. But all was just the same as it had been except for the bowl of oatmeal in her hand.

"It is fairy meal then," said Jean to herself. "Well, I have never tasted fairy meal before, so I shall make some porridge for myself now, just to find out what it tastes like. The Fairy Folk! Dear me! I have heard my mother talk about them many a time. She said they live in this part of the land and that they always dress in green. They dance in fairy rings under the moon on summer nights, I have heard her say. She has said too that many a time they visit folk like us and sometimes they do them harm and sometimes they leave them gifts. Well, if I had known that the beggar woman was really the Queen of the Fairy Folk, I would have been more polite to her! She might have given me a golden penny for the meal I gave her!"

All this time Jean was making the porridge. But she did not use all the meal in the bowl. That would have been a shameful waste, she thought, for just one person. So she hid what was left on the high shelf behind the teapot where she kept her gold crowns.

"I will put the rest there," she said. "I don't mean to tell John anything about it, or about the fairy boy in green. If I did, the foolish man would be wanting to put a bowl of porridge on the hearth every night. He would leave it for the fairies to eat if they chanced to come here. Some folk do that, I have heard, just to keep the Fairy Folk in a good temper! But I am not going to have such a waste of good food going on in my house!"

When the porridge was ready, the miller's wife sat down to eat it. Oh, how good it was! She had never tasted such nice porridge in all her life!

"Well," said Jean aloud as she went on eating

spoonful after spoonful, "the Fairy Folk know how to grind good meal, I must say. But what a pity it is that their Queen did not pay us back in gold instead! Gold! Oh, there is nothing like it! How I wish we had sacks and sacks of it! Yes, I wish that all the grain ground in this mill would change into gold instead of turning to meal and flour. Oh, what a fine treasure I should have then! I wish I could have gold around me always, wherever I went. How happy I should be!"

The Golden Millstone

It was late when the miller got home the next morning. So, as he had a lot of grain to grind, he went straight to the mill before going in to see his wife.

John quickly set the mill wheel, ready to grind grain. But how great was John's surprise when, on looking to see whether the flour was coming, he saw no flour at all! Instead, there fell from the wooden trough shower after shower of golden coins!

At first John stood stock-still staring in amazement. Then he put more corn into the mill—

as much as it would hold. Still, it was just the same. Nothing but gold coins came out instead of flour—hundreds of coins, and oh, how brightly they shone! Soon they were all over the floor of the mill, lying here, there and everywhere just like gleams of sunshine.

The miller was about to run into the house to fetch his wife when a voice at the door cried:

"What is the matter, John? What has happened to us? Take this great stone off my neck! Oh dear! Oh dear!"

There stood Jean in the doorway. She was holding fast to the doorpost to keep herself from sinking down. For round her neck was a great heavy millstone made of gold!

"Oh, oh!" cried Jean again. "What shall I do? This great thing has been round my neck ever since I woke this morning! I cannot get it off, try as I will, and the weight of it is so terrible I can hardly move!"

The miller's wife was in such a state that she scarcely noticed the shining coins that lay all over the mill floor. At any other time, she would have cried out in joy at the sight of so much gold.

John did his best to get the great golden stone off

his wife's neck, but all in vain. Whatever he tried he could not move it. At last, exhausted by carrying the great weight, poor Jean had to be helped back into the house.

The wishes she had spoken aloud as she ate the fairy meal had come true. From that hour, all the grain ground in the mill turned to gold instead of flour and meal. And from that hour, Jean had gold around her—a dreadful collar of gold—wherever she went.

Fairy Gold

At first, John was very pleased to think that now he now a golden mill, as he called it. "For that is surely a golden mill which grinds out golden coins instead of flour or meal," he said.

"A sack of gold is worth more than a sack of flour. Now I can give sacks of gold to all the poor people I know. How glad they will be!"

That evening an old man came to the mill with some corn which he wished to have ground into flour. John took it, set his mill to work and ground it, and in a short time the old man had two sacks of gold instead of flour. Full of wonder and delight, he set off for home with his prize.

"Oh, how lucky you are," he said to John, "to have this golden mill! Why, you will soon be the richest man in the land!"

"Perhaps I shall," said John. "But remember, there will be plenty of gold for everyone. Come again when you want some more."

Before sunset he had given away more sacks of gold. He gave one to a poor farmer's wife, two to a lame ploughman, who had ten children, and three to a beggar who passed the door.

It was a good thing that Jean was not there to see him giving away gold like this. It would have been a dreadful shock for her! But Jean stayed indoors all the time, moaning with pain, with the golden millstone round her neck. Would she have to wear it always? What a terrible thought that was!

But before breakfast next morning, the old man came again to the mill with his sacks.

"What!" cried John as soon as he saw him. "Have you spent all the gold I gave you yesterday?"

"Oh, neighbour," said the old man in a sad tone, "I did not think you would play such a trick on me! See what I found when I opened my sacks of gold this morning!"

And opening one of his sacks, he showed the miller that it was filled to the brim with nothing but yellow dust!

With a loud cry, John ran into the mill and opened the sacks that stood there. Every one was filled with dust and nothing else. There was not a single golden coin to be seen anywhere!

Then along came the farmer's wife, the ploughman and the beggar. All three were very angry at the trick they said John had played on them. For they too had been cheated. Their sacks were now full, not of gold, but of dust.

Poor John did not know what to think about this strange thing that had happened. "It is not my fault," he kept on saying; "I did not mean to cheat you—no, not for a moment! I thought I was giving you good gold money; I did indeed!"

"I will tell you what it is," said the old man at last. "It is the work of the Fairy Folk. Your gold is nothing but fairy gold which turns to dust. Well, I am sorry for you, neighbour. Your golden mill is no good to you after all!"

The Miller's Wishes

For some time, things at the mill were in a very sad state. Jean took no pleasure in anything for the terrible golden millstone weighed her down night and day, and she could not get rid of it. As for poor John, he shut up his mill at last and locked the door and would not go near the place.

So for weeks the great mill wheel was still. No one brought grain to be ground now, and the miller would not grind any for himself either. What was the use? The fairy gold was no good to anyone. It would not buy anything; it would not even keep long enough to be looked at, for every bit ground each day turned to dust in a night.

One day it was found that the meal in the meal chest was all gone. "You will have to go and buy some more, John," said his wife, "since you cannot grind any. There are some gold coins in my old teapot on that shelf. Take one of them; they, at least, will not change to dust. They are not fairy gold. Gold! Ugh! I wish I had never seen it! I hate the very sight of it, that I do!"

Now, when John took the teapot from the shelf, he saw the bowl of fairy meal which his wife had hidden. "Why," he cried, "there is nearly a bowlful of meal here!"

"Oh, John, don't touch it!" cried Jean. "It is fairy meal. It will do us more harm if we taste it—all our troubles have begun since I ate some of it."

Then she told her husband all about the visit of the boy in green and about the porridge she had made from the fairy meal. She told him too of the wishes she had spoken as she ate it.

John thought for a long time and at last he said:

"I am going to make some more porridge from the fairy meal and I am going to wish, as you did, when I am eating it. Then we shall see what will happen."

"Please yourself," said Jean. "I shall have nothing to do with it."

So John made the porridge and began to eat it. He had no sooner swallowed the first spoonful than he cried out aloud:

"Oh, how good it is! How I wish that my mill would grind meal as good as this and good flour too every day as long as we live! I wish that we could live as we did before, content and happy, with just

enough for ourselves and something to spare for
other folk as well! And I wish that poor Jean had no
golden millstone round her neck!"

As he spoke these last words, his wife gave a loud cry and began to dance with glee. John looked at her in wonder; and then he too gave a cry of joy. For the golden millstone had gone!

The miller's other wishes also came true in a very short time. Soon the mill was grinding the best flour and meal in all the land. John was very glad, for now he had always enough and some to spare for his poorer neighbours.

Jean too, was now very happy, and she was as ready to give as her husband had always been. She was mean no longer, nor did she now care for gold, for the Fairy Folk had taught her a lesson which she never forgot. And whenever any poor or sick or hungry folk needed help, they were sure to find it at the Golden Mill.

The Old Oak and the Seven Sisters

"It is very tiresome that we have to live next door to that oak tree," said a silver birch, one fine spring day. She and her sisters were looking very charming as their tiny round leaves and graceful catkins quivered and shook in the breeze. There were seven of these pretty birches in a little group close to the old oak—some people called them the Seven Sisters. With their silvery white bark, slender trunks and drooping branches they were like dainty dancers on tiptoe waiting for the signal to take the next step.

The oak was very, very old. Many things had happened to him during his long life and he bore many scars. Long ago one big branch had been struck by lightning and it still stuck up, gaunt, ugly and dead above the surrounding trees. Many smaller branches had died or been torn off by storms. Yet still when spring came round the sap stirred in the twisted old trunk and the tree put forth new leaves.

The birches seemed to shiver with disdain when their sister spoke of the old tree.

"Anyhow," said one, "we need have nothing to do with him. No one takes any notice of the old bore nowadays."

"Oh dear!" exclaimed one of the others suddenly, "I do wish that rabbit would stop eating my bark. It tickles and leaves ugly marks."

"I wish," sighed another, "I wish birds would build nests in my boughs."

"No, thank you," said the first. "Nasty, messy things! Anyhow, our branches are not safe enough."

The old oak listened to their chatter. He felt rather lonely, but he had his memories and thoughts to keep him company. He knew that oak wood is of great value for making furniture and many years ago, England's ships. He remembered how his own branches, when strong and full of leaves, had sheltered many birds which had nested and reared families. All the same, he was lonely now. The idle chatter of the birches was worrying. They never seemed to be still either, always fluttering and quivering as if they might take flight. Where should I be today, thought the oak, if I had not grown sturdy and solid with a fine depth of root?

As the moon rose, a tawny owl flew into a tree near

the Seven Sisters. She was a brown bird with large round eyes and a hooked beak. She sat crying strangely, "Oo-oo-oo". She was looking for a place to build a nest. She turned her gaze towards the birches. "Too flimsy," she decided. "I need a nice deep hollow safe and cosy. Oo-oo!" she cried with pleasure, for she had just seen the oak. "The very thing!" Flying to the oak she found an ideal hole

halfway up the trunk and a convenient branch made a doorstep. She lost no time in claiming it for her home.

The word must have got round that the old oak was a good place for a home. Mrs Tawny Owl had no sooner laid her three white eggs than a pair of jackdaws came to build a nest near the top of the tree. There was a cranny too where they hid any bright oddments they found. Their amusing chatter and cry of "Jack, Jack, Jack", kept the old oak entertained. A woodpecker now came daily to the tree for a favourite kind of insect which she found under the bark. Her loud, laughing voice was enough to cheer anyone!

At night, Mrs Tawny Owl went hunting, calling "Ki-wik, ki-wik". She would hunt for young rabbits, squirrels, weasels or even fish if she caught any swimming near the surface of the water. The strange thing was that, though she would catch an unwary bird such as a blackbird at night, she would never trouble them in the day. Indeed, in daylight they would sometimes fly at her when she sat peacefully dozing near her hole!

When the young birds had flown, the oak thought he would now feel his loneliness even more. But as autumn came, he was pleased to find that various small creatures had discovered the cosy holes around his roots and were preparing to take up residence. A family of hedgehogs stowed away in a fairly large hole into which a lot of dead leaves had drifted, making a snug bed for their winter sleep.

Some mice had the hole next door and a dormouse climbed a little way up the tree to take a very old bird's nest for his cold-weather home.

So the oak tree settled contentedly down for his winter sleep. The sap stopped flowing to the gnarled old branches; the leaves fell to add another layer to the deep carpet at his feet. He was no longer lonely. He was no longer useless, because surely it was worth something to be giving shelter to the small, trusting animals who had chosen him for their home. He could not help thinking, as he glanced at the Seven Sisters, that they looked very bare and chilly, trembling pale and leafless in the sharp autumn air.

The Coloured Carriage

His Majesty the King of Krumpley had a fine, large and exciting-looking carriage. It had the most expensive-looking ornaments. The cushions on the seats were so soft the King seemed to sink right into them. There were tassels round the coachman's box and little steps at the back for footmen to stand on. The harness on the horses had bells on it which tinkled as the carriage went along, and feathery plumes which waved in the wind.

But in spite of all these pleasant things, the King

of Krumpley was unhappy about his carriage.

"Gold carriages are a bit common, you know," he said to the coachman. "I mean, everyone has a gold carriage—every king. I think I ought to have a carriage quite different from any other carriage."

"What say we paint it red, Majesty?" suggested the coachman, who was handy with a paint brush and didn't mind splashing paint about now and then.

"Good idea," said the King. "I am graciously pleased to be pleased. Let the carriage be painted red."

"Yes, Majesty," said the coachman. So he went away to let it be painted red, which he found meant painting it red himself. It also turned out to mean painting himself red here and there, because he was rather careless with the paint.

"Lovely," said the King, when he saw his carriage all gleaming scarlet. "That's what I call a most kingly carriage. Drive me out in it."

He stepped in, and the coachman drove off. Tinkle, tinkle went the bells. Wiggle, waggle went the plumes. Clopetty-clop went the horses' hoofs, and zim, zim went the wheels, all going round the same way as they were meant to do.

But they hadn't gone far when round a corner burst another red carriage, even redder than the King's. And it had louder bells. It was a fire engine.

"Bother it all," said the King, trying to stamp his foot, but finding he was too far sunk into the cushions to be able to. "Home at once, and let the carriage be painted blue instead. I couldn't dream of having my carriage the same colour as a fire engine. The very idea!"

So home they went, and the coachman got busy letting the carriage be painted blue by painting it blue himself.

"Beautiful," said the King, when he saw it. "Much more royal looking than a mere red carriage, I'm sure. Drive me out in it."

Off they drove with the bells tinkling, the plumes waving, the horses clopping and the coachman with a nice round blue smut on the end of his nose, but that wasn't supposed to be there.

But, oh dear, dear, they hadn't gone more than a street or two when down the hill came roaring a most vivid blue carriage, simply stuffed with policemen of all sizes. And this carriage had no bells to tinkle, but all the policemen were blowing whistles, which more than made up for it.

They were chasing a most dishonest person who had stolen a flower out of someone's front garden.

"Tut, tut," said the King. "This is awful! I simply cannot have my carriage the same colour as a policeman's van. People will think that I've been arrested, or else they will stop me to ask the time. Home, coachman! Let the carriage be painted green."

In a day or two the royal carriage was a lovely green. So were both the coachman's ears and several of his whiskers.

"Delightful," said the King. "Drive me out in it."

But they were hardly outside the Palace gates when they were almost run into by a most brisk and brashy carriage also painted a beautiful green. And this had no bells, no whistles were being blown and there weren't any plumes. But there was a very loud little boy sitting on a lot of baskets at the back, making assorted faces at people as they shot past. It was a laundry van.

"Disgraceful!" stormed the King, climbing out of the carriage so that he could stamp his feet on the pavement. "I refuse to have a carriage the colour of a laundry van. I shall be accused of losing people's

shirts. Everyone with a torn handkerchief will blame me. Let the carriage be painted yellow."

"Yellow's a bit like gold in colour, Majesty," said the coachman, who was beginning to think he had done enough painting for a bit.

"Purple, then," shouted the King. "I will not have a carriage the same colour as anybody else's, so there."

At last the royal carriage was painted purple, and the coachman to match it, because he was getting very careless with the way he sloshed the paint brush about.

But, oh dear, tut, tut indeed, and fancy now. The King was just getting into the carriage for a drive when there shot by another purple carriage. And this purple carriage had no horses even, let alone bells or whistles or plumes. And it was being pushed rapidly along by a heavy gentleman calling out that he wanted rags, bottles and bones.

That did it more than ever. The King was so furious at the idea of having a carriage like a rag-and-bone-man's cart that he stalked back to the Palace and wouldn't eat his tea.

"What colour next, Majesty?" asked the coachman, putting his head round the door.

"Red!" shrieked the King.

"It was red last Tuesday and matched the fire engine," said the coachman.

"Blue!" stormed the King.

"Same as the police carriage," reminded the coachman.

"Green!" roared the King.

"Laundry," said the coachman.

"Dark black with assorted spots then," yelled the King, bringing his fist down on a bun which happened to be a creamy kind of bun and shot a splodge of cream into his eye. "Let the carriage be painted some colour it hasn't been yet," he commanded, "and if any other carriage is the same colour, off with your head."

"Dear, dear," thought the coachman, who was quite tired of painting the carriage any colour at all, but definitely disliked the idea of having his head chopped off. "Now what can I do?"

He went miserably back to the carriage house and stared at the carriage. And the more he stared at it the more he didn't like it much. Then his eye fell on the tins of paint he had been using. Suddenly, he had an idea—a silly idea, but still an idea.

All that day the carriage house was firmly closed, and when the coachman came out he went straight off and had a highly special bath in different kinds of strong-smelling liquid to get the paint off himself, because there was a great deal of paint on him, and a great deal of him for there to be paint on.

"The carriage is ready, Majesty," he said, when he was fairly clean again.

"What colour?" asked the King.

"If Majesty will be graciously pleased to drive out in it, I think Majesty will be graciously pleased to be pleased," said the coachman. He took out his handkerchief to blow his nose. And he not only blew his nose, he also made his nose blue, for there was some paint on his handkerchief where he'd wiped his painty hands.

The King stepped outside to see the carriage.

"Good gracious!" he exclaimed, and his eyebrows went up to different heights.

The carriage was neither red nor blue. And it wasn't yellow, or purple, or green, or pink. And yet it was. Yes, yes, it was all colours at once—in dots and

squares and stripes. It was so highly coloured you could almost hear it coming without the bells on the harness.

"Drive me out in it," commanded the King. And off they set. And although they met many a blue or red or green or purple carriage, not one single vehicle of any kind had so many colours as the King's carriage.

"Splendid!" said the King. "I am pleased with you and I shall give you a nice present."

The King's present turned out to be a nice new box of paints, but the coachman was so absolutely tired of the sight of paint, whether on himself or other things, that he took it secretly back to the shop and changed it for twenty tins of toffee.

Ahmet Saves the Day

Once upon a time there was a little girl called Fatima who lived in a village in Turkey. Little Fatima had a cow called Bridie. One morning Fatima was milking the cow and accidentally kicked over the bucket which was full of milk. The milk spilled all over the floor.

Fatima was worried and afraid because if her sister Ayshe learned she had spilled the milk she would be very angry. Then Fatima had an idea. She took off the necklace of gold coins which she wore round her neck and put it round the cow's neck.

"My beautiful Bridie," she said to the cow, "my

gold necklace is now yours, but don't tell my sister that I upset the bucket and spilled the milk, will you?"

Bridie nodded her head, as if to say, "Very well, I won't tell."

Suddenly the stable door opened and Fatima's sister Ayshe came in. She was very surprised to see the gold coins round the cow's neck.

"Fatima, what does this mean?" she asked.

Fatima couldn't tell a lie so she explained what had happened.

"While I was milking, my foot hit the bucket and knocked it over. The milk in the bucket spilled out. I gave my gold coins to Bridie so that she wouldn't tell you about the spilt milk."

When Ayshe heard this she too became afraid, because if her mother heard of the spilt milk she would be very angry.

So she took off the silk head scarf she was wearing and draped it over the cow's head.

"My beautiful Bridie," she said to the cow, "my silk head scarf is now yours, but don't tell my mother that my little sister Fatima spilled the milk, will you?"

Bridie nodded her head, as if to say "Very well, I won't tell."

The stable door opened again and Fatima's mother came in. She was surprised to see the gold coins round the cow's neck and the silk head scarf over the cow's head.

"What's the meaning of this?" she asked her elder daughter. Ayshe didn't want to tell a lie so she explained what had happened.

"While Fatima was milking the cow her foot hit the bucket and knocked it over. The milk spilled out of the bucket. Fatima gave Bridie her gold coins and I gave her my silk head scarf so that she wouldn't tell you about the spilt milk."

Their mother became afraid too, because if her

husband heard of the spilt milk he would be angry. So she took her lace shawl which she wore around her shoulders and laid it on the cow's back. "My lace shawl is now yours," she said to Bridie, "but don't tell my husband that Fatima spilled the milk, will you?"

Bridie nodded her head, as if to say, "Very well, I won't tell."

The stable door opened once more. This time it was Fatima's father. He was surprised to see the gold coins round the cow's neck, the silk scarf over her head and the lace shawl on her back.

"What's all this?" he asked his wife.

As she didn't want to tell a lie, so she explained. "Our little Fatima hit the bucket with her foot and knocked it over. The milk spilled out of the bucket. Fatima gave Bridie her gold coins, Ayshe gave her the silk head scarf and I put my lace shawl on her back so that she wouldn't tell you about the spilt milk."

Father didn't want his son, Ahmet, to hear all this as Ahmet was to inherit the household. If he heard about the spilt milk he would be very angry. So Father took out his silver watch and chain from his pocket and tied it round the cow's middle. Then he said to the cow, "My beautiful Bridie, my silver watch and chain is now yours, but don't tell my son, Ahmet, that Fatima knocked over the bucket and spilled the milk, will you?"

The cow nodded her head as if to say, "Very well, I won't tell."

The stable door opened yet again. This time it was Ahmet who came in. Ahmet was just as surprised to see gold coins round Bridie's neck, the silk scarf over her head, the lace shawl on her back and the silver watch and chain round her middle.

"Father, what are all these for?" he asked.

His father also did not want to tell a lie so he explained to his son what had happened. "While she was milking the cow, your little sister Fatima accidentally kicked over the bucket. The milk spilled all over the floor. Fatima gave Bridie her gold coins, Ayshe gave her the silk scarf, Mother gave her the lace shawl and I gave her my silver watch and chain so that she wouldn't tell you about the spilt milk."

Ahmet listened carefully to the explanation. Then he thought about what it could all mean, but he couldn't make any sense out of it.

"All this is very confusing," he said to himself. "I can't possibly live with such stupid people. I must find myself another village."

So Ahmet put some food into his saddlebags, took up a stick, threw his saddlebags over his shoulder and set off to find a village where sensible people lived. There he would make his home.

After a while he came to a village. "This is a nice village. I'll stay here," he said to himself.

At the gateway to the village some men were gathered on the road. In the midst of them was a donkey. They were trying to load a sackful of grain on to the donkey, but when they put the sack on to the donkey's back it kept falling off. They tried various ways but they couldn't load the sack on to the donkey.

Ahmet said to them, "Load both sides of the donkey so that it balances. Then the sack won't fall off."

They did what Ahmet suggested. They weighed the grain and filled another sack with the same weight of stones. Then they loaded one side of the donkey with the sack of grain and the other side with the sack of stones.

But the donkey couldn't carry the load as it was now too heavy. And it fell down on to its knees.

Ahmet said to them, "It's useless to load the donkey with stones. Separate the grain into two parts and divide it between the two bags."

They did as Ahmet suggested and put half of the grain in one sack and the other half in the other sack. Then they loaded the two sacks on either side of the donkey and it began to move forward shakily.

When they saw this, the villagers said to Ahmet, "You're a very clever lad. Settle down here in our village and help us always with your cleverness."

Ahmet replied, "I can't possibly live amongst such stupid people as you." And he set off again on the road.

After a while he came to another village. This village also looked pleasant. "This is a nice village, I'll stay here," he said to himself.

People had gathered in the centre of the village. A young man was on the roof of a house and on the ground below stood two men holding open a pair of breeches.

"What are you doing here?" Ahmet asked them.

"That young man on the roof is trying to put on his breeches," they replied.

At that moment the young man jumped off the

roof down towards his breeches, but he missed and fell on to the ground and hurt his head.

"You don't put breeches on like that," Ahmet cried.

"Then how do you put them on?" the villagers asked.

Ahmet took up the breeches and showed them how to step into them in the usual way.

"Now that's very clever, young man. Settle here in our village then you can help us with your cleverness," said the villagers.

"I can't live among such stupid people as you," Ahmet cried, and set off on the road again.

Some time later he came to another village. This looked a really nice village. "Whatever happens, I'll stay here in this village," he said.

In the village that day there happened to be a wedding. At the head of the wedding procession rode the bride seated on a pony. The bride had just arrived at the door of the house where the wedding would take place. The relatives wanted to get her through the door still mounted on the pony. They tried and tried but they couldn't get her through.

Someone said, "Let's cut off the horse's legs, then we will get the bride through."

Another said, "That won't work, we can't cut off the horse's legs. Maybe we should cut off the bride's head!"

Thinking they were about to do this, Ahmet threw himself forward. "Stop!" he cried. "I'll get the bride inside for you."

Ahmet then hit the bride on the head with his fist and the bride bowed her head with pain. As she

lowered it the pony and the bride together went through the door.

On seeing this the villagers said to Ahmet, "You're a bright lad, settle down in our village then you can help us with your cleverness."

But once again, Ahmet said, "I can't live amongst such fools as you," and he set off again.

Ahmet travelled far and wide but nowhere could he find a better village than his own. So finally he set off for home.

When he arrived back he went straight into his house. There he found that his family had filled the room with water and made a pond in the house. They had made a boat out of the cow's feeding trough and were all sitting in it, including Bridie the cow.

Ahmet was bewildered. "What are you doing?" he asked.

"My brave young son," answered his father, "since you left our village, we've been sailing around in this trough."

"Yes, but what are you doing in the trough?" Ahmet asked.

"We're looking for you," answered his father.

Ahmet smiled and said, "Yes, it's best in your own village, and as it's my own, here I must stay."

And his mother, father and sisters all embraced him and welcomed him home.

Annabelle

In the olden days, in a distant country far away to the south, there was a rich merchant. He lived in a big house close to a wood just outside the city.

He had a lovely daughter whose name was Annabelle and she was the most skilful seamstress in all the land. She could make gorgeous robes,

exquisite gowns, beautiful dresses and all manner of wonderful things, and she could do the most delicate embroidery on the finest of fine silk with threads so fine that you could hardly see them.

When she had made all these beautiful things, she put them away in a big oak chest in preparation for her wedding day which was to be very soon, for she was engaged to be married to a handsome young man who lived in the city. His name was Julian and they were deeply in love with each other.

On her wedding day—the first day of spring—Annabelle, like all other brides, was careful to wear:

Something old,
something new,
something borrowed,
something blue.

She put on her beautiful new wedding dress of snow-white satin and under it she wore two petticoats of the finest of fine silk–a white petticoat and a blue petticoat. She had a beautiful old veil which her godmother had given to her, and just before she left home she borrowed a fine silver needle from her closest friend and tucked it into the hem of her wedding dress, where no one could see it.

Then leaning lightly on her father's arm, she set off, followed by all her friends, for the great church in the city where Julian was waiting for her.

Suddenly, just as they were halfway to the church,

a brigand on a big black horse dashed out from behind a copse of trees by the roadside. He seized the lovely Annabelle, tore her from her father's arm,

dragged her on to his saddle and galloped off with her. In a few moments they were lost to view.

Riding hard for many days from dawn until sunset, he carried her to a distant country in the north, far away beyond the mountains. At last they reached his great stone castle on top of a hill in the heart of a forest.

"And now," snarled the brigand, "now you shall be my bride or you will regret it for the rest of your life!"

"Villain!" cried Annabelle, "villain! I will never consent to be your bride, whatever you may do."

"Ha, ha! my proud beauty!" growled the brigand, "ha, ha! then I shall lock you up for ever." And he

dragged her off to a turret high up on the castle wall, thrust her into a tiny cell and locked the door with a big brass key. There was only a little square hole in the wall of her tiny cell to let in some daylight and there were iron bars across it so that she could not escape.

When he heard how Annabelle had been snatched from her father's arm and carried off by the brigand, Julian was overcome with grief. But that very day he set off on his beautiful white horse, and for many weeks rode and rode over all the countryside, through the fields and forests, across plains and over

mountains, seeking news of Annabelle. But there was no trace of her. No one knew where the brigand had come from or where he had gone, and finally, in despair, Julian had to return home.

Day after day, week after week, Annabelle sat in her tiny cell, weeping and weeping. The only company she had was a swallow which flew in one day through the little square hole in the wall and made its nest in the rafters.

Annabelle was so gentle and so quiet, that the swallow grew quite tame and had no fear of her. She loved to talk to it as it sat on its nest or rested on the end of her bed, but she knew that quite soon, when summer drew to a close, the swallow would leave her and go back to its home in a distant country, far away to the south.

"A distant country!" thought Annabelle, suddenly. "A distant country far away to the South! Perhaps even to my own country. I will get the swallow to carry a message for me, and the message might fall into the hands of someone who knows me, and who will rescue me—perhaps even into the hands of Julian himself!"

For the first time in many weeks she was excited and happy, and she remembered the fine silver needle she had tucked into the hem of her beautiful wedding dress of snow-white satin.

Quickly, for there was no time to lose, she tore a small piece from her fine white petticoat and with her skilful fingers she drew out the white silken threads one by one by one–threads so fine you could hardly see them and she threaded her fine silver needle.

Then she tore a tiny piece from her fine blue petticoat with the white silken threads she embroidered a message on it, and the message was just one word. It was her own name—Annabelle.

Gently, very gently, and quietly, very quietly, she crept up to the swallow as it rested on the end of her bed, and, with one of the white silken threads, she tied the tiny piece of blue silk to the swallow's wing.

That very day, as the sun went down, the swallow left its nest and flew off to its home in a distant country far away to the south. On its wing was a tiny piece of blue silk with just one word on it—Annabelle.

The swallow flew and flew for many days, until, on the last day of summer, it reached its home in a distant country far away to the south, and it came to rest in a garden.

On that very day, Julian was walking sadly in his garden, and his heart was filled with grief and sorrow. Then by chance he saw a swallow resting after its long journey from a distant country in the north, far away beyond the mountains. To his great surprise, he saw that a tiny piece of blue silk was tied to the swallow's wing with a white silken thread and he wondered what it could be.

Quietly, very quietly, he crept up to the swallow. Then gently, very gently, he picked it up–for it had grown quite tame–and took from its wing the tiny piece of blue silk, and, to his astonishment, he saw there was something on it.

He looked again and his heart leapt with joy, for there, on the tiny piece of blue silk, embroidered with white silken threads, was just one word—Annabelle.

Just one word, but it was all Julian needed to drive away his grief and sorrow, and for the first time in many weeks he was excited and happy.

He knew the swallow had come from a distant country in the north, far away beyond the mountains. He knew now that somewhere in that distant country was his own dear Annabelle. He determined to go at once and rescue her.

Quickly, for there was no time to lose, he prepared for a long journey, and that same day he set off on his beautiful white horse.

Riding hard for many days from dawn until sunset he came, at last to that distant country in the north far away beyond the mountains.

Day after day he rode through all the countryside, seeking news of Annabelle, but in vain. He rode to every city, every town and every village, but there was no trace of her. Wherever he went he called out

"Annabelle! Annabelle!" but there was never an answering call, and he was in despair.

One day, as the sun went down, he came by chance to a great stone castle on top of a hill, in the heart of the forest. He was weary and very sad, but he rode up to the castle, calling out "Annabelle! Annabelle!"

Suddenly, from a turret, high up on the castle wall, there came an answering call, "Julian! Julian!" He called out again, "Annabelle! Annabelle!" and again there was that answering call, "Julian! Julian!" There could be no mistaking that clear, sweet voice and he knew he had found at last his own dear Annabelle!

His weariness quite forgotten, Julian rode up to the gates of the castle and demanded to be let in. But the brigand laughed in his face. "Go back!" he snarled, "go back to your own country far away to the south or I will come out and cut off your head!'

Julian was fearless, and he was determined to rescue his Annabelle. Drawing his mighty sword, he battered down the heavy gates of the castle and rode into the courtyard.

There stood the brigand, armed to the teeth, and in the fading light they fought so fiercely that the clash of their swords could be heard throughout the forest.

First the brigand was struck down, then Julian. First one seemed to be the victor, then the other. The fight went on, but as darkness fell, Julian gradually gained the advantage, and with one last blow of his sword, he struck the brigand down and cut off his head!

Swiftly Julian took the big brass key from the brigand's belt. Then he rushed into the castle and up the dark stone stairs–up and up until he came at last to the turret high on the castle wall where Annabelle was imprisoned.

With the big brass key he unlocked the door of her tiny cell, and his heart was filled with joy as he was

reunited with his own dear Annabelle. He took her in his arms and kissed her again and again and again. Annabelle wept but her tears were of pure happiness.

On the following day they left the castle, and for many days they rode, side by side, until they came at last to their own country far away to the south, and to their own city.

Annabelle was overjoyed to see her father once again, and he embraced her with special tenderness, for she was his only child and very dear to him.

With happiness in her heart she once more made preparations for her wedding day, and very soon everything was ready. Annabelle put on her beautiful wedding dress of snow-white satin, and below she wore her two petticoats of the finest of fine silk–the white petticoat and the blue petticoat. She did not forget the beautiful old veil which her godmother had given her and, just before she left home, she again borrowed the fine silver needle from her closest friend, and tucked it into the hem of her wedding dress where no one could see it.

Leaning lightly on her father's arm, she set off, followed by all her friends, and walked to the great church in the city where Julian was waiting for her.

There they were married amid great rejoicing and lived happily ever after.

Princess Miranda

In the olden days there lived a King and Queen who had a daughter called Princess Miranda. She was the most beautiful princess that ever lived and all the young knights and nobles at the King's court fell deeply in love with her.

One day it was Princess Miranda's birthday. In the evening the King and Queen were giving a magnificent ball at the royal palace. They invited all the young knights and nobles at the King's court and all the young maidens who lived in the city–all except one–the daughter of a wicked witch and the ugliest maiden in the whole city.

All that day, and far into the evening, the wicked witch sat by her smoky fire. She bit her nails and wondered what she could do to cast an evil spell upon Princess Miranda. Suddenly she had an idea!

She remembered she had a magic book hidden up the chimney. So she stretched her long skinny arm up the chimney and brought down her book.

It was indeed a wonderful book! On one page there was a spell for turning handsome princes into toads.

On another page there was a spell for turning rich ladies into snakes. There was a different spell on every page but right on the very last page she found the spell she was looking for.

"If," it said, "you can shoot Princess Miranda right through the heart on a moonlit night, she will be turned into a bird. And a bird she will remain forever."

This was just what the wicked witch wanted. The moon was shining brightly that very night, so she clapped her hands three times, and in came her old cat with his tail up. His name was Black Tom.

"Black Tom," she said, "I have a magic bow, and I've hidden it up the tallest tree in the wood. Run and fetch it for me." So he scampered off with his tail up, climbed to the top of the tallest tree in the wood and brought the wicked witch her magic bow.

"Thank you, Black Tom," said the wicked witch. "Now I have a magic arrow and I've hidden it down the deepest well in the city. Run and fetch it for me."

He scampered off with his tail up, climbed right down to the depths of the deepest well in the city and brought the wicked witch her magic arrow.

The wicked witch took the magic bow in her left hand and the magic arrow in her right hand. Then she got on her broomstick and flew off into the night. Round and round she flew until she found herself right over the royal palace.

At an open window, Princess Miranda in a white robe stood gazing at the starlit sky.

The wicked witch swooped down, and drawing the magic bow, took aim and shot the magic arrow. It struck Princess Miranda right through the heart and down she fell.

At the very moment the arrow struck, the princess turned into a beautiful snow-white swan. Hopping on to the windowsill, it opened its great wings, rose into the air and flew off into the night to a faraway country.

That very same night, the prince of that faraway country was out in the forest hunting by moonlight He was the most handsome prince that ever lived.

Suddenly he heard the beating of wings overhead. He looked up and saw a beautiful snow-white swan flying through the sky.

Swiftly he drew his bow and shot the beautiful snow-white swan right through the heart. Down it dropped from the sky and fell at his feet.

At the very moment the swan touched the ground, it turned into a beautiful princess dressed in a white robe. It was the Princess Miranda herself.

The prince fell instantly in love with her. Going down on one knee, he took the princess in his arms and kissed her. But alas! the wicked witch had cast her most powerful spell on the princess. In a few moments she turned once again into a beautiful snow-white swan.

The prince, overcome with grief, drew his dagger and plunged it into his heart.

Down he fell by the side of the beautiful snow-white swan.

At the very moment the prince touched the ground, he too turned into a beautiful snow-white swan. Together the two swans opened their wings, rose into the air, and flew off into the night, and lived happily ever after.